Dinner Table Distractions

Addison Gordon

Illustrated by Renata Smagulova

Young Authors Publishing

Young Authors Publishing
www.youngauthorspublishing.org

Book Design by April Mostek

Our books may be purchased in bulk
for promotional, educational, or business use.
Please contact Young Authors Publishing by email at
info@youngauthorspublishing.org.

This book belongs to

_____

Dedication

Mom, I want to dedicate this story to you:
thank you for letting me help cook dinner,
and it always makes me happy.
You taught me to never give up,
even when something goes wrong.

Addie lives in a small village in San Francisco, California. She lives with her mom Selena, her dad Fred, and her little sister Luci. Addie loves spending time with her family.

Addie loves to cook with her mom. Her favorite thing to cook is pizza! She likes chicken, spinach, and extra *extra* cheese on her pizza.

"Yum!" she exclaims every time.

When Addie's family sits at the table to eat their meal, they are always talking! There isn't a single phone in sight.

"How was your day?" mom questions.
Everyone begins talking at once!

After dinner, Addie puts the dishes in the sink while her parents wash them.

"Let's go play, Addie," Luci screams, before tagging Addie and running outside.

Now, Addie is in the sixth grade and her parents are both entrepreneurs, which means they own their own businesses and are extremely busy. Luci is in the fourth grade and their days are filled with school and homework.

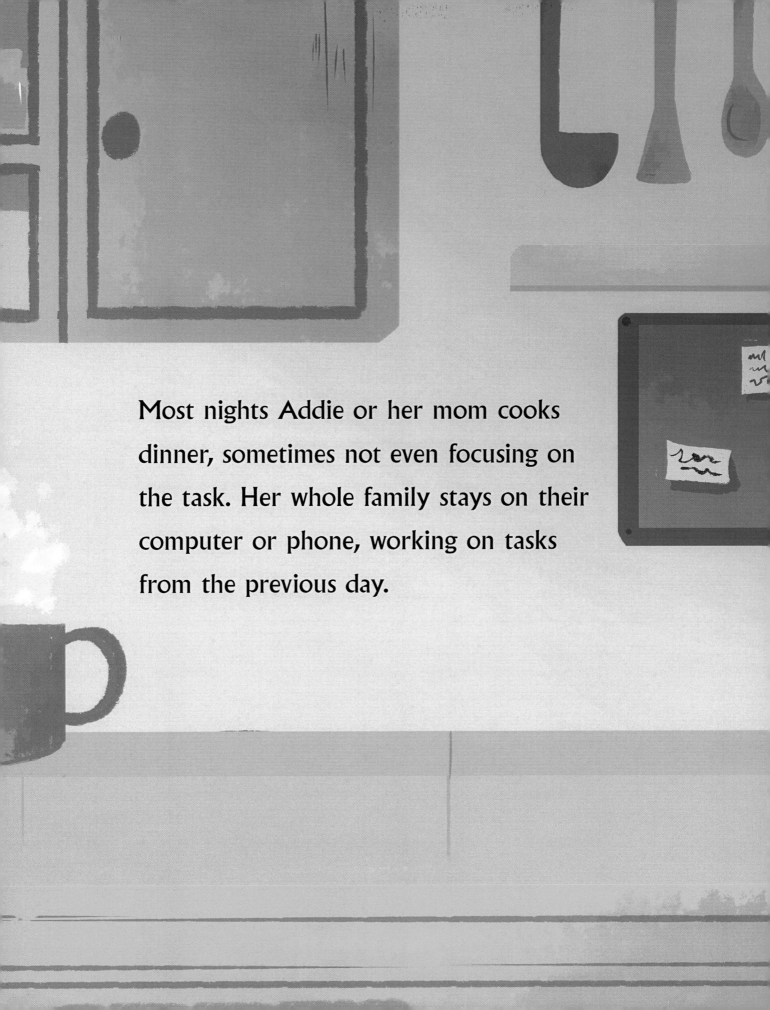

Most nights Addie or her mom cooks dinner, sometimes not even focusing on the task. Her whole family stays on their computer or phone, working on tasks from the previous day.

One day during lunch, Addie and
all her friends talk about where they
went out to eat last night.

"I had to go pick up food with my
dad again while everyone else stayed
at home and worked," whines Addie.

When Addie gets home she sees everyone working. Throwing herself on her bed, she thinks about how times have changed and now everyone seems too busy to spend time together.

"I wish my family could spend more time together—what can I do about this?" ponders Addie. Drifting asleep, she thinks about a day when her family can spend quality time together again.

The next morning,
Addie decides to call
a family meeting.

"We need to have some family time around here! I want to have a nice dinner where everyone is talking and no one is on their phones." Addie shouts in a loud voice.

Slowly everyone nods their heads yes. "Yeah, that sounds great!" her mom agrees.

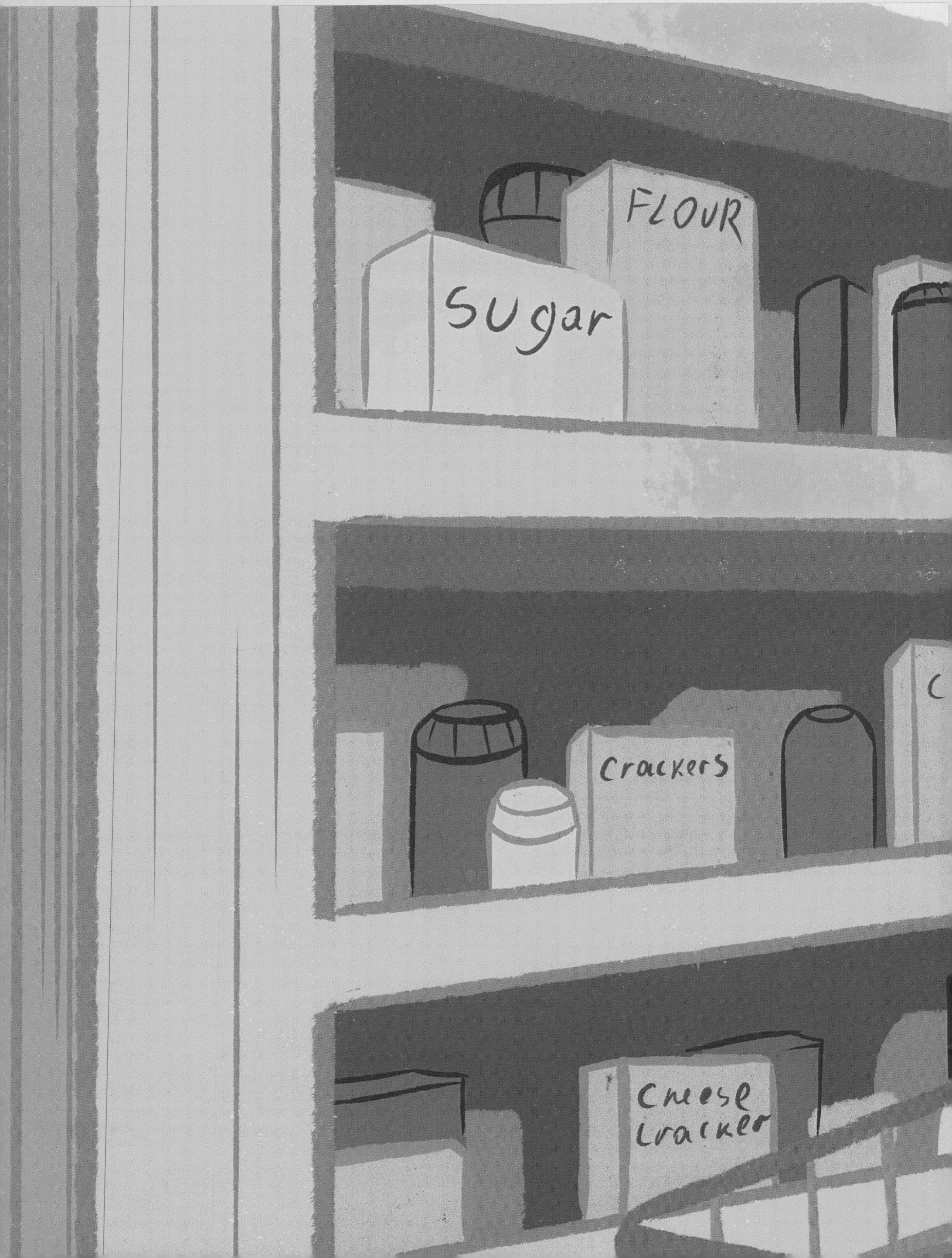
FLOUR
Sugar
Crackers
Cheese Cracker

Later on in the day, Addie's family goes to the store to buy ingredients for the pizza. Everyone begins to argue about what they want on their pizza.

"I want pepperoni on mine!" Addie exclaims.

"No, I only want cheese on my pizza!" Luci says.

When they get home, Addie and her mom make the pizza. They toss the pizza extra high in the air and the dough falls flat on Addie's head.

"Oh no! Now we have to start all over," Addie screams.

"It's okay, we have more pizza and toppings to make," her mom laughs as she lifts the dough from Addie's head.

FLOUR

On Monday Addie goes back to school
and tells her friends what she did.

"My family and I had a big meal
together, with no distractions,"
Addie says happily.

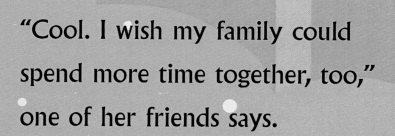

"Cool. I wish my family could
spend more time together, too,"
one of her friends says.

"Spending time with your family
is important," Addie states.

From then on, Addie and her family eat dinner with no distractions, and they have enough time for each other every night.

"I'm so happy that I get to spend time with my family again!"

Addie and Mom's Pizza Recipe

INGREDIENTS

Thin crust refrigerated dough

4 small cups of tomato sauce

4 medium cups of shredded mozzarella cheese

1 pack of pepperoni

STEPS

1. Heat oven to 425°F. Spray a large cookie sheet with cooking spray. Place the dough on the cookie sheet and start in the middle. Press into a round circle. You should bake for 9 minutes.

2. Spread the pepperoni on one side on one side of the pizza and leave the other side blank. Then you should bake the pizza for 8 to 10 more minutes until the pizza crust is golden brown.

That is Addie and Mom's pizza recipe.

About the Author

Addison Gordon is ten years old; she has a younger sister who is three. Her favorite things to do are play the piano and violin, sing, and practice gymnastics. She likes to cook with her mom, and when she's older, she hopes to be a chef and own her own bakery where the specialties will be biscuits and cake.

ABOUT YOUNG AUTHORS PUBLISHING

We believe that all kids are story-worthy!

Young Authors Publishing is a not-for-profit children's book publisher that exists to share the stories of children, many who live in underrepresented communities. Young authors participate in our Experience Program where they are paired with a trained writing mentor who helps them write their children's book. Once their manuscript is complete, young authors learn the fundamentals of financial literacy, entrepreneurship and public speaking. When you purchase a book from Young Authors Publishing, you're helping a child write a new story and change the narrative.

OUR FAVORITE PART!

Eighty percent of all the book royalties are deposited into a secured savings account for each young author to use toward their post-secondary plans.

Learn more about our impact at www.youngauthorspublishing.org

YOUNG
AUTHORS
PUBLISHING